Tales from the Canyons of the Damned

DANIEL ARTHUR SMITH

Tales from the Canyons of the Damned No. 17

First Edition

Special thanks to Jessica West

ISBN-13: 978-1946777324 ISBN-10: 1946777323

Cover By Daniel Arthur Smith

Horror Fiction from Holt Smith ltd
Agroland
Tower

~*~

For Susan, Tristan, & Oliver, as all things are.

~*~

103 Days
D.K. Cassidy

~*~

IN 103 DAYS I'M RETIRING. Not sure if that's a good thing. Having nothing to do might be dangerous for me. Being a nurse is all I've ever known. My identity, my world.

Boarding the ferry this morning, she began her countdown to—what? Helen wouldn't call it freedom. More like forced solitude. No friends outside of the hospital, the people she worked with were acquaintances.

A non-existent life outside of work had never been revealed to them. If you asked any of Helen's coworkers, they'd tell you about her vibrant social life. They'd be shocked to see how she really lived. Her only companions: books, television, and, of course, her papa.

Looking over the railing of the ferry, the same she'd commuted on for years, Helen watched for dolphins.

I see one! It's a sign I'll have a good day.

Superstition had always been a way of life for her. The older she grew, the more superstitious she became. Fountains called to her to toss in a coin and make a wish.

Black cats weren't allowed to cross her path. She avoided leaning ladders at all costs. Her precious father instilled these beliefs in her impressionable mind.

~*~

When she was a child Helen's father gifted his daughter with his view of the world. A place of magic, wonder, and luck. He taught her the rituals that guided her even now. Salt over the shoulder was the first one. After that, he instructed her to avoid cracks in sidewalks, and told her about the magic of certain numbers. She remembered the first time she made a wish on a falling star. Helen didn't tell her papa her wish because he told her it wouldn't come true if she did. So instead, she whispered it to herself.

I wish my papa would never leave me.

"Papa why are black kitties bad luck? They're so cute. I wish we could have one."

"Don't worry about why, Pookie, just remember what I teach you. Someday when you're older, I'll read you some of the stories my mother passed on to me."

"Ooh look, we have to cross the street. That sidewalk is all cracked. We need to keep mama safe."

"Good girl, you're learning. Time to go to the store and get ingredients for stew. We don't want to keep your mama waiting."

~*~

Believing she needed to bank some good luck, today was the start of a new ritual. Opening her bag, Helen pulled out the first token of luck and tossed it into the water, but not before taking a photo to post on Instagram. Her younger co-workers taught her about the world of social media. It still fascinated her how people shared everything with strangers, but now here she was doing the same. She wondered what her followers would think of her first post. Maybe she'd trend.

~*~

Helen continued her daily commute to work every day thereafter, depositing her tokens each time she rode the ferry. As she tossed each piece into the water, she felt a burden lifting from her. She was doing the work she'd been meant to do. As she had on the first day of this ritual, she posted a photo of the token on Instagram. Some of the tokens were large, others quite small, but all were of equal importance.

Her followers grew swiftly. By day 59, she had 35,000 followers. People she didn't know and would never meet. But they had one thing in common: her photos. Helen learned about hash tags and meticulously tagged each photo to gain more followers. She wished to share her joy with the world, but also wanted to remain anonymous. She used an avatar of a nurse for her photo and a fake name. Worried her coworkers wouldn't understand what she was doing, she'd told none of them about her account.

But there was a man at work who wanted to be her friend. Barry. Every few days he asked her out for drinks, but her reply was always no. He followed her on Facebook. Helen knew her instinct to have an anonymous Instagram account was right. Barry would follow that account too if he knew about it.

"Hi Helen! I liked your post about tides. You seem to know a lot about them," said Barry.

"I ride the ferry every day so I notice them. When I was younger..."

"Hey you're not that old."

"As I was saying, when I was younger I used to go digging for clams with my mama and papa. Actually, my mama didn't like to get sand in her sandals, so it was papa and I who got the clams. She made chowder for us."

Barry looked surprised by her long answer.

"I think that's the most you've ever said to me at one time, Helen. Maybe there's a chance for me?"

As he said this, he was looking down at her phone. When he walked away, Helen noticed her phone was open to her Instagram account.

~*~

Back at work the next morning, Helen chatted with a co-worker.

"Hey Helen, did you see what I posted on Facebook last night?" Sarah asked.

"No, sorry, I was busy. What was it?"

"The comet! NASA says there's an enormous comet coming, and it's headed toward Earth! It's been all over the news. The scientists say it'll be here in a couple of weeks."

Helen put on her best concerned face and answered.

"That's scary news, Sarah. Where's it going to hit?"

"The scientists seem to think it'll land in the ocean, but what if it hits a city? Our city?"

A buzzer sounded at the nurse's station, interrupting their conversation.

"That's Mrs. Garland in room 242, got to go."

Helen watched Sarah hurry to the patient's room and decided it was her duty to help Sarah and the world feel safe, and not worry about the comet, but wondered if her luck would be strong enough.

This will take extra good fortune. I'll make a wish when I drop my token into the water on the way home tonight. Papa always says doubling up creates extra protection.

A tap on her shoulder disturbed Helen's thoughts.

"Some of us are going out after our shift today. Interested?" Barry asked.

"No thank you, my father needs me."

"Is he sick? You haven't mentioned him for a while. If you're worried I'm asking you on a date, that's not what this is about. Just coworkers getting together."

"He needs me, that's all. My papa gets lonely; he never got over the death of my mother ten years ago. Have fun tonight."

"What about you, Helen, don't you ever get lonely?"

At the end of her shift, Helen boarded the ferry and stood in her spot next to the railing on the car deck. She leaned over, waiting until they were half way across. It was time. She took out the next token and dropped it into the water. No photo today, she was on an important mission, and documenting it on Instagram this time seemed shallow to her. She needed to focus on stopping the comet.

The rest of her commute consisted of a short drive to her house. Helen ignored the dilapidated look of her house and her overgrown herb garden. Time. There wasn't enough of it for her to spend on outward appearances. Most important to her was what or, rather, who, was inside: Papa.

"Hey, Papa! I'm home! Today was a good day at work. None of my patients died today. I'd call that lucky wouldn't you? Why is it so quiet in here?"

She realized she forgot to turn on the television before she left that morning. Her papa could not do that for himself. Helen felt the twinge of guilt that surfaced when she thought she'd failed him.

"So sorry, Papa. Let me turn on the television for you. There's big news. A huge comet is heading this way. Now don't fret, I'm going to fix it. I'm making extra luck."

The rest of the evening was spent in amiable silence. Papa propped in front of the television, Helen cleaning her tokens. She skipped cooking dinner; Papa didn't want anything to eat.

~*~

Barry was waiting for her outside the nurse's changing room. This made her nervous, although she wasn't sure why.

"Um, Helen, could we talk? I need to ask you about something."

"I'll be late for my shift in the ICU, Barry. Can this wait?"

"No, it won't take long. I really have to find out more about what you've been posting."

"I haven't put anything up on Facebook for a couple of weeks now. Been too busy."

"No, not Facebook. I found your Instagram account and there's something strange about it."

"Why are you looking at my account? I don't want any of my coworkers following me there. Now leave me alone, you freak!"

"But the photos. I don't understand the photos."

Helen walked away without answering him, furious he'd invaded her privacy.

~*~

At the nurse's station, those not with patients were staring at the television. Before Helen continued to the ICU, she watched the news.

"In breaking news, the comet identified yesterday as headed toward the earth has changed its trajectory. Scientists remained baffled at this course change and will continue to study the comet."

Helen smiled. Her tokens were bringing luck to her and the world. Bursting to tell someone, she remained silent. It was better not to take credit for this miracle. Papa wouldn't want her to brag.

~*~

At the end of her final shift as a nurse on day 103, Helen dropped the last token into the water. A flat neck tie shaped bone called the sternum. She watched it float briefly then sink to join the other 205 tokens, one for each trip to and from work: the culmination of her papa.

~*~

Keep Rolling
Jason LaVelle

~*~

A MONKEY. A dead fucking monkey.

"Dammit," Kendra whispered, hunching over the furry black creature. She looked from side to side nervously. The cameras were mounted everywhere in these woods, they had definitely seen it. *This is going to look bad.* Kendra, a generally warm and fun-loving woman and well-known animal lover, worked as a veterinary assistant back home. Yes, this was going to look bad.

Kendra sat back on her haunches, thinking and scratching at her arms as she did so. Red, welted fly bites covered her arms and, in fact, her whole body. On her third day in the jungle, she'd slathered thick brown mud all over her naked body, trying to throw the bugs off her scent. It had worked, kind of. The mosquitoes had stayed away, but the mud contained some kind of mites that proceeded to bite at her most tender parts: beneath her pubic hair, in her armpits, and down through her butt crack, anywhere that was hot and sweaty. For days afterward she had been scratching her crotch and ass like a baseball player. Kendra gave up on the mud after that and let the insects feast on her body.

Her ears picked up movement above and her head snapped up. She imagined she looked like a feral animal, crouched down next to the dead howler monkey, her knees pulled up with her arms around them. She looked into the trees. The morning sun was shining down through the canopy, rendering everything above her into silhouette, making it impossible for her to see any real detail. They were up there, though, she knew it.

She heard a soft hooting noise, then another.

"I didn't mean to!" She called up, oblivious to how ridiculous she must look on camera. "It was an accident!"

In response, something wet showered down on her, splashing into her short dark hair and over her chest. *What the...* She wiped a hand over her dirty breasts then raised it up to her nose. Piss. They had pissed on her. She heard a loud screech, followed by several more, and soon the whole canopy above her was screaming. Kendra pressed her palms against her ears, but the noise was still deafening. She squeezed her eyes shut and concentrated on breathing. *In and out, nice and slow, find your center.*

She had been alone in this jungle for two weeks, surviving on palm hearts and berries that she hoped to god weren't slowly poisoning her. She'd begun to adapt to the loneliness, and even to the constant itching of insect bites. But the slow starvation was changing her. Weakness consumed her muscles. Even walking a dozen steps away from camp to urinate drained her energy. Animal lover or not, she needed protein, she needed meat.

That's why she set the rudimentary snare. She hoped to catch a rabbit or rodent of some kind. Not a monkey. Even for this show, which was broadcast live to millions of viewers, the monkeys were off limits. The Black

Howler Monkey was on the endangered species watch list, and all *Naked Warriors* had strict instructions not to harass them. It was an accident, though. She couldn't be held accountable for that, could she? With her eyes closed, Kendra's breathing finally slowed. Then something thick and foul hit her in the face. *No, they wouldn't...*

Kendra wiped her face and came away with a smear of sticky black and green tar. Now that was just too much.

"No, fuck you!" Kendra screamed up at the monkeys. Her face was smeared with shit, and her body shook with anger as she pointed up at them.

"I didn't mean to kill it, but now he's mine!" She shouted, then angrily grabbed the dead howler off the ground. She stripped the snare off its neck, then held it up above her for the others to see.

"I'm taking him," she shouted, waving the twenty-pound mass of fur and muscle above her head.

The multitude of monkeys in the canopy howled in rage. They shook the trees and threw more excrement at her, but Kendra smiled up at them. To the cameras she probably looked a bit mad, a wild creature with a body sunken from hunger and dehydration, her ribs protruding awkwardly below breasts that seemed to be deflated.

She forgot about the show for a few moments, about the fifty thousand dollar reward she would earn if she stayed in this damnable jungle for thirty days. For the moment, at least, she was consumed with a feral and frightening excitement. She held the dead monkey tight by the neck and took off, running through the jungle. The howlers followed, screaming at her the entire way. She didn't care. Kendra ran for ten minutes until she reached her camp. When she finally got there, she was sucking in deep, heavy breaths of humid air. Her legs hurt and trembled under the effort.

Her shelter was a rough lean-to, a skeleton of thin branches covered by layers of long palm leaves. It was only big enough for her to sleep in, but that was all she needed. She was pleased to find her fire still smoldering in front of the shelter. Kendra tossed the monkey to the side and stirred up the coals, causing heat to rise thickly. She added small pieces of dried bark that she had scavenged, and a few moments later flames started to lick their way over the wood.

The troop of howlers rustled the trees directly overhead. Kendra could feel their foul rain coming down, but she was beyond caring now. A kind of savagery had overtaken her, and it seemed to only be inflamed by the sight of the dead primate—of a fresh kill—of food. She hadn't eaten meat in weeks, and though she was too dehydrated to salivate, her mouth hung open, ready to taste it.

She picked up her machete. The long blade was one of the two items she'd been given for this test: that and the fire starter. Grabbing the monkey and a flat rock, Kendra looked to the screamers overhead. Then she flipped the monkey onto the rock and raised the machete. She brought it down with all her strength, decapitating the dead animal instantly and chipping the rock beneath it.

With a mad gleam in her eyes, Kendra picked up the head and hurled it into the canopy above her, screaming a warrior cry as she did. She expected an immediate response from the monkeys, but they went silent. Kendra turned in a circle, looking all around. The monkeys weren't moving around, but she heard the hum of cameras tilting and panning up in the trees, watching her.

She swiped the monkey carcass and held it in front of her, toward one of the cameras.

"Now I have meat!" she screamed into the camera, and bit down onto the monkey's bloody neck.

That was a terrible idea. Kendra gagged immediately at the metallic taste of blood and let the mouthful of red warmth dribble off her chin and over her filthy body. She picked hair out of her mouth. *Of course I have to cook it, of course.*

Using the machete again, she sliced open the hairy black bundle and peeled the skin from its body. Then, she scooped out its organs, grimacing as she squeezed too hard and received a rancid burst of ichor from its bowels. *Shit that's gross, like getting anal gland fluid right in the face.* Once the monkey was naught but muscle and bone, she tossed it onto the fire. Her mouth curled into a smile as the meat heated up. It smelled like heaven. After two minutes, the monkey began to sizzle. She could practically taste it now, like a nice cut of beef, a tenderloin, seared and grilled just enough to take the cold edge off, juicy and tender and rich. She flipped the monkey over to cook its eviscerated underside.

A *whoosh* sounded through the jungle above and something hard hit her in the back.

"Ah!" she cried out. *Jesus, that really hurt.* She looked around the ground and found a golf-ball sized rock. Those little bastards had thrown it at her.

"Nice try!" she shouted and threw the rock back up into the leaves. She turned back to the fire and another projectile sailed through the forest. This time she heard it hit some leaves and tried to duck, but it struck her in the knee. Kendra immediately fell over and a bright splash of pain washed through her. The rock had struck her on top of the patella bone. Her entire leg felt numb. No, not numb, she was in too damn much pain for that. Her lower leg felt fuzzy and wouldn't respond to her commands, while her upper leg and knee throbbed in agony.

"Goddammit!"

She tried to cry, but had no tears. Another rock sailed toward her. She flung her hand out to protect her face, but the rock found its mark anyway, and struck her in the corner of her mouth. More pain bloomed, and her vision wavered for a moment. She gagged and coughed and a gob of blood with a broken white shard of tooth leaked out onto the forest floor.

"You!" she screamed. "You a-holes!"

Kendra crawled over to the fire and plucked the monkey out. It was cooked now, and the aroma of its grilled flesh was wafting through the jungle. She held the searing hot monkey in one hand and took a huge bite of its thigh, as if she were eating a drumstick.

"Extra fucking crispy bitches!" she shouted through a mouthful of monkey meat.

More rocks came, faster now. They struck the ground all around her, landing with little *thumps*. Several struck her body, but she kept eating, ripping huge chunks of monkey off the heavy morsel. Then sticks started coming down at her. The first were light, but they quickly increased in size, and then one with a jagged end came down with a soft whistle. The shard of wood pierced her thigh, sticking out of her like a throwing knife. She cried out and scuttled back—right into the fire.

Kendra jerked and spasmed, trying to get off the fire pit, finally rolling to the side. The fire had scorched her nether regions, burning off pubic hair and searing the tender flesh below.

"Oh shit, oh shit that hurts!" She rolled onto her side, holding one hand between her legs. She started to sob, a tearless, awkward thing, her whole body shaking. She was curled in a fetal position, trying desperately to stomach the new pain. *Just be strong, you can do this!*

Then the largest stone so far sailed through the forest and struck her spine. She felt and heard something *pop* in her back and suddenly the pain between her legs was gone. In fact, she couldn't feel her legs at all.

Oh my god, am I paralyzed?

She didn't have long to think about it. The howlers started screaming again, and now she heard thumps and scurrying all around her. They had come down from the canopy. Kendra picked her head up and tried to crawl away, but her legs were like dead weight, and all she could do was army-crawl on her elbows. Her machete was nearby, if she could just get to it…

Thump, right in front of her. She looked up into the bald face of a large, male howler monkey. It was about two feet tall, tiny compared to a human, but the furry beast was solid muscle. Its mouth opened and closed in a gnashing motion, showing off its four long, sharp incisors, yellowed with age. The monkey reached down to its side and picked up her machete. It held the knife like a person would, with thin fingers wrapped around its handle. It was amazing how human-like these creatures were, but Kendra didn't feel awe, she only felt fear.

The howler stared at her with small, dark brown eyes, holding her machete. Then something warm and heavy landed on her back, knocking the wind out of her. Strong fingers dug into Kendra's hair and held her up. They were strong, so very strong. The animal on her back gave a soft hoot, and the monkey in front of her screeched. It looked down at the machete in its hand, then back at Kendra. She thought she saw a smile on its tiny black face, and then it lunged at her with the blade.

~*~

14

"Holy shit," the technician whispered. The room was quiet and dim as they watched the howlers slowly tear the woman apart on their main screen. A red light blinked overhead, telling them that they were still live. "What should we do?"

"This is the best show we've ever had," his supervisor answered. "Keep rolling."

~*~

Hazard to Navigation
Jon Frater

~*~

"TAKE A GOOD LOOK, MY DEAR. We won't get another chance."

It was almost like a camping trip. They'd left their house an hour ago and driven to this spot off a country road just to watch the big event. No trees. No lights. Just the two of them.

Emma pulled the blankets closer around her to ward off the January chill. The hood of Sam's pickup did not make the most comfortable way to watch the night sky, but they'd been blessed with clear weather. Almost no clouds. And, luckily, no wind, either. Just the full moon beaming its face down at them.

"How much longer?" she moaned. "My fingers are turning blue."

He checked his watch. "Should be soon. Midnight. Assuming they mark time the way we do."

"Midnight is what the observatory geeks told us. I assume they'd know. It's their job."

"Right." He opened the thermos, poured a few ounces of hot coffee into a plastic cup, offered it to her, then poured another for himself. "Think they'll still have jobs after tonight?"

She snorted. "Why not? The stars will still be there. And we know a lot more about them now."

"I guess." Sam gulped his coffee, wincing at the heat, then settled against the truck's windshield. "What if there were no moon?" he asked. "What then?"

Emma drew her legs up, sitting cross-legged. "Well, no tides, for one thing. Darker night skies, for another."

"How about earthquakes? We'd still get those?"

"Sure. But the moon doesn't really influence earthquakes." She paused to think. "Now, if it suddenly vanished, then you'd get earthquakes. Big ones. Tidal waves, too."

"What'll the werewolves do?"

She punched him in the arm. "No moon, no werewolves. Duh."

He peered through the binoculars he'd hastily packed as they left the house. Sharp lines cut across the lunar face, barely visible once he focused. "Can't see the crater."

"Check the north quadrant. Just above the crater Plato."

Sam followed her instructions. "Nothing. We'd need a proper telescope for it."

The breeze picked up. She snuggled closer to him as he let the lenses fall against his chest and put his arm around her, bringing her in. "It'd be weird, not seeing a moon."

"It would. There's nothing in the solar system quite like it. We're not even sure where the damn thing came from. I like to think we wouldn't miss it."

"But we would," Sam nodded. "You miss anything that suddenly isn't there. Hell, people freak all over when their cell phones run out of juice. Forget PCs, laptops—oh my god, when the electricity or plumbing quits..."

She sighed. "Yeah. There'd be a panic. We'd go crazy for a while. But we'd get used to it. We get used to everything. War, disease, famines, crushing poverty…"

He checked his watch again. "Five minutes. I'm really burned that we can't see the crater from here."

"Come on. Even if you could, the wreck is long gone. We had to return it. They were very specific about that."

"Think we should listen on the radio? President should be on by now."

"You can listen if you want. I don't care."

Sam rolled off the hood and turned the key. The engine rumbled to life. He figured Emma would appreciate a warm hood. He turned the radio on and found the station. POTUS was indeed on the air.

"The moon. It's a hazard. It really is. The biggest hazard to life we've ever seen. You know the dinosaurs? An asteroid got them. A big one. But as big as that was, the moon is a billion times bigger. That's billion with a b. I've made a deal with our nearest neighbors to do something about it. Because I'm a deal maker. It's what I do. And when the Virani scout ship crashed, we were shocked and terrified. But then, their diplomats contacted us and said, hey, America, your moon is a hazard to space navigation. I said, fine, let's do something about it. And they will. Because I made that deal with them. Very nice people, the Virani."

Sam turned the knob, killing the voice. "I think we've heard enough of that."

Emma pointed upwards. "There!" she squealed. "It's starting."

They couldn't see the Virani ships despite their size. A glint of reflected sunlight was all Sam found through the binoculars. But the beams they projected were brighter than the sun, lancing out from lunar orbit, searing the surface of the massive satellite to glass, then pulverizing the surface. As they watched, the surface of the moon faded, blurred to a silver-gray cloud.

Emma frowned. "We might get a ring out of this. Depends on how much material is left when they're done."

"Well...a ring would be cool! Right?"

She snorted. "It'd be different. But I don't think it would capture the imagination of future generations."

They stayed and watched. The cloud grew in size, fuzzing at the edges, like a fantastic faerie ring. But the faeries were working in ships a mile long and from a distant solar system. And despite the president's broadcast words, there was no deal to be made. The Virani had lost a ship and demanded corrective action. The big men who ran the world took no time to recognize that the visitors could evaporate the surface of the Earth as easily as they were now doing to its only satellite.

A shot rang out. Then, two. Down the road, headlights appeared in a column.

Emma rolled off the truck's hood and joined Sam in the cab. "We should go back," she said.

He nodded, and started the engine. "Yeah. People are going to go crazy."

~*~

Hugo King vs The Many Menacing Minions of the Malevolent Menace Doctor Chicago

Paul K. Swardstrom

~*~

MY NAME IS HUGO. HUGO KING. You wouldn't believe the day I've had. It all started…

"Who are you talking to Hugo?" the head beside me asks. The head belongs to Glory, my girlfriend. She used to have a body—until this morning.

"I'm just engaging in some internal dialogue, dear." I explain.

"Well, it's hurting my toes. Stop it."

I roll my eyes. She doesn't have any toes.

"I do too! We're just having a temporary separation right now. Can you drive any faster?"

I nod and gun it.

"And stop the internal dialogue. My toes ached a bit harder

when you denied their existence just now."

I sigh, trying very hard not to roll my eyes. I reach over and flip a switch on the base of the machine keeping her head alive. I watch out of the corner of my eye as her eyes droop sleepily.

"You scum, Hugo King!" she protested as consciousness faded. "When I get out of this thing I'm going to kick your..." Her voice stops working altogether as she drops off to sleep.

I smile wryly as I speed on to her underground lair. What a day indeed. Let me tell you about it.

Wait a minute.

I reach for the sports drink in the cup holder that has just a little bit of something extra. Don't judge. If you'd had the day I've had... Anyway... deep breath...

I had a commercial shoot this morning in the store, King Tronics and Appliances. You know the place - where Huge-o $avings are the word... I'm sure you've heard of it. My face is plastered all over town in every newspaper ad section, at the bus stops, billboards, radio and TV commercials...

Have you heard of my other businesses? King's Mattress City or King's Furniture Emporium?

Do you live in a cave?

At any rate, we just finished a take and the director was looking at the footage when Glory burst on the scene. It ended up being the last take because when Glory shows up nothing else matters—at least in her eyes. She's the kind of girl who is hot in such a way that she knows it. Whatever room Glory walks into is her space whether everyone else realizes it or not.

"Hughey!" she exclaimed as she glided into the room in her high heels and sequined dress, "I absolutely have to talk to you."

I was peering over the director's shoulder at the moment— a little guy named Spellington. He seemed brilliant with the camera and could always capture just the right angle. I looked up while he squinted his eyes and slammed headphones over his ears. Spellington knew Glory all too well. She'd been the 'talent' for some productions he'd been in charge of. However, he was trying desperately to shake her like a bad habit.

Her entrance was, well, glorious. What can I say? She knocks my socks off every time. She is also devoted solely to me, which I thank the Good Lord for every morning, right after I thank him for my good looks and my daddy's good business sense over my morning Cheerios. Then I thank the Good Lord for my penthouse, the mansion, the two vacation houses and my favorite car. Isn't she a beauty? Just look…

Oh yeah. You're reading, not watching. Well she's a beauty and, aside from Glory, I value her the most. I named her Kitty because of the way she purrs at idle. She can get from zero to sixty in 4.3 seconds, all leather interior, the most amazing stereo system…

Sorry. I go off on tangents sometimes. Anyway, back to the action. Glory stormed in and I could see immediately that we would need some privacy.

"Hughey!" she said again, "I need your help, and I need it now." She added a little stomp for emphasis and batted her beautiful eyes at me.

I sighed and looked over at Doris, my personal assistant. "Looks like I'll need you to postpone the meeting with Sales. Move it to…" I glanced back at my anxious girlfriend, "Tomorrow. While you're at it clear my slate for the next couple hours…" I checked again. She was chewing her fingernails and looking left and right. "Make that the rest of the day. This looks urgent." Glory relaxed, slightly.

I took her arm in mine and waved over at Tom, my business manager. I could count on him to pick up the slack for the day, something he'd had to do on a couple of occasions recently, but never for nearly an entire workday.

He gave a thumbs up and a wink and I felt a little better. Hopefully he wouldn't be able to orchestrate a corporate coup in the next six to eight hours.

We walked back to the corporate office wing behind the main floor showroom. My electronics and appliance business had four locations in the greater Westport area and suburbs. This location on 28th Avenue was the site we had chosen to create our headquarters. My granddad's original store was just down the street, a resale store now.

We walked down a corridor littered with photographs of me—meeting this celebrity or that celebrity, shaking hands or in half-held hugs for the camera. My favorite pictures were those of players on my favorite basketball team—The Razors. I kept those on the wall just outside my office.

On the way, Glory chatted me up conversationally about my morning so far, "How did the morning go? How was the shoot? Did you have something clever to say? Did you have a special guest star? What were you trying to sell? Do you need me to help you with any talent?" But as we entered my office, Glory turned and firmly closed the door.

She paused for a moment, and when she turned to face me, I could see that she was shaking.

"What's going on, Baby?" I came in close for a hug. She seemed to thrive on affection, and I loved to give it to her. This time, however, she pushed me away.

"He's coming," she whispered.

"Who?" I whispered back. I didn't know what was going on. Perhaps a jealous ex? And why was she whispering?

She paced around the office, holding her head in her hands—the irony in that is just catching up to me right now. She was talking to no one in particular, just going on with some kind of crazy internal dialogue. Here's an example, "He's found me. He's going to get me. It's not good when he catches you. That's when the experiments happen. The pain, the torture, the tickles, and the rabbits! The Rabbits!"

I still have no idea what the rabbit thing was all about. After watching Glory rant like this for what felt like an eternity, but was more likely just a few seconds, I walked to where she was and grabbed her by the shoulders.

"Glory!" I spoke loudly at her. It didn't have any affect. What was going on here? She was fine just a few seconds ago. I shook her shoulders and raised my voice. No effect. She kept mumbling and tried to stumble around me. I didn't have a choice really. Recalling movies made in the early part of the last century, I slapped her cheek, hoping it would snap her out of it.

"What?" She seemed dazed and a bit surprised. She looked up into my eyes. "Did you slap me?" she said with her most endearing voice.

"Yes," I responded. "You were catatonic. I didn't hav—" I didn't finish that sentence. A well placed knee in the jewels took care of that. I grabbed the closest chair and sat down, doubled over in pain.

"Oh, Hughey, did I hurt you?" She bent down to my level, now filled with concern. I was not appreciating the effort at the moment. "I'm sorry. It was an automatic defense protocol—if slightly delayed. Apparently my systems were fuzzed up enough that it didn't respond at the right time, but it did respond at your vocal confirmation."

"What the heck are you talking about?" I asked in a weak voice, still doubled over on my chair. "You're not making any sense. None at all since we stepped into this office."

She smiled hesitantly across the small gap between herself and the comfy chair that held my huddled form. "It's Doctor Chicago. He's finally found me, I'm afraid." Glory paused for dramatic effect. "I'm afraid that my time here on this planet is over—one way or another."

I stood slowly. I was still aching in the num nums, but I could see that Glory needed some sense talked into her. "Did you take some weird medication or have some food poisoning?" I asked. "You're not making any sense."

In response, Glory simply pressed on her collar bone with both hands. I heard a click, a sigh, and then she picked her head and neck right up off of her body. She held it there, staring back at me for several seconds while I quickly reassessed my own earthly existence. I'm pretty sure the expression on my face was about the dumbest look I've ever had because then she started laughing.

"Calm down, Hughey. It's ok. Haven't you ever seen a disembodied head before?" She winked.

I didn't know how to respond, but I did want to get a better look. I started circling around her while she was talking. "I, uh, guess so," I responded. "But that was always a TV show or movie."

"Well that wasn't always fake, Hughey. Sure, the head in a box on a table is fake, but this—this is real." She held her head out so I could get a better look. I could see how it would snap in— gaskets at the base of the neck must connect to the body. I could see bulges in the bottom reflecting the movement of muscles in the neck. I didn't understand everything I saw, but it was clearly beyond the technology of Earth at present.

"Are you human?" I asked.

"Yes… and no," she answered as she slid the head back in place and locked it in. "Most of me—" She didn't get to finish because at that moment the door slammed open.

My head jerked at the noise. "What the…" I started. Glory pulled my arm back and pointed at the floor. I could see indentations in the carpeting coming toward us. We continued to back up and put the desk between us and the indentations. My mind was having trouble coping at the moment, but there was obviously something there, I just couldn't see it. We backed around my desk, and I realized that I wasn't completely defenseless. I opened the drawer, grabbed a can of silly string left over from the last office party, and sprayed it. As I did, I took two more steps back and grabbed the baseball bat I kept as a trophy behind my desk.

The formerly invisible creature charged as I sprayed so I didn't have much time. It leapt over the desk and made a beeline for Glory. It didn't care about me. Perhaps it didn't know I could see the silly string it was trailing. As it came over the desk I swung around one handed with the bat and chopped at what I hoped was the head as it went by me.

It only took that one swing. The invisible monster, now partially covered with silly string, went down. I looked over at Glory, plastered in the far corner. "Are you ok?" I asked. She gulped and nodded.

We turned our attention back to the creature on the floor. At first I thought I must have had the luckiest shot in history because what looked like blood was seeping out of it, causing it to be more visible, at least in the area that was being covered by the blood. It appeared to be a gorilla mask, because no actual living thing could look that bad, could it? But then, I saw the twitch of the cheek and the flutter of the eyelid, and I knew that as ugly as that thing was, it was real.

I turned back to Glory. I don't know what my face looked like but I was still feeling a mix of surprise and shock, now augmented by the mortal danger presented by the ugly invisible gorilla monster. Perhaps Glory had some answers. After all, she was the one with the removable head. "You're full of surprises today. Do you know what the heck this thing is?"

"I've heard of creatures like these," Glory said. "They're supposed to be unstoppable in their pursuit. I don't understand how you took it down so easily."

I hooked the bat over my shoulder and smiled my most endearing smile. I know it's endearing because my commercial director, Steven Spellington, told me so. "Well, if you need any more monster bashing, you know where to find me."

And then I felt it, a cold sensation creeping up my ankle. I backed away fast and looked down. The blood from the invisible ape was following me. I could see Glory backing away as well. We both freaked out and bolted to the other side of the desk. It was simple instinct. If you discovered that some kind of blood was climbing up *your* leg, I bet you'd freak out too.

Arriving on the other side of the desk we heard the sound of liquid sloshing from the floor behind us. I had a sinking feeling. Glory was already pulling my hand toward the doorway. I let myself be pulled while I continued to watch what was unfolding. In another moment, a large form slinked over the top of the desk. This gelatinous blob paused, somehow seemed to orient itself and then oozed toward the door where we were standing.

I felt a yank on my arm. "Let's GO Hugo!" Glory implored me. It snapped me out of my daze. I dropped the bat and turned to follow after her, but not before shutting the office door. I didn't know how fast a creeping blob of jello could open a door or extrude around it, but I was betting it wasn't quick.

We bolted into the hallway, where I pulled the fire alarm. I didn't want the employees in danger, right? We closed every door we passed on our way out of the building. I would have loved to make some more substantial blockade, but I didn't feel like we had the time.

We made it down two flights of stairs and out to the back parking lot. I could see people streaming out of every exit, but I made a beeline to my speedster Kitty with Glory at my side. I turned the key while Glory put on her seatbelt. I smiled at the loving purr from Kitty and patted the dash. I backed out, ready to gun it, but I hesitated when my desk landed on the pavement in front of me. I should have taken off then, but curiosity overcame me. I could feel Glory's grip on my arm tightening, but I was paying more attention to what followed the desk out of my third story window.

Calling it a Frankenstein would give it too much credit. The gelatinous goo had found enough office furniture and equipment to construct a makeshift skeleton. It seemed to descend in slow motion, although that was probably more my own senses trying to capture the totality of the beast rather than a true slow descent.

Made up of an amalgamation of equipment found in the third floor office suite, I saw table legs creating the bone structure of the arms and legs, toasters from the break room for feet, a metal coatrack for a spine, staplers for fingers, and the security cameras from the hallway outside my office suite in the place where you would expect the eyes to be. It looked incredibly awkward—a toddler still learning to walk. But lumbering with an uneven gait, it sure moved faster than the goo that tried to crawl up my leg in my office.

The goo/office equipment monster landed ten feet in front of the car and immediately turned its camera eyes to us. I couldn't wait any longer. I shifted into reverse, turned to look over my shoulder, and peeled out.

The office and warehouse staff were standing around the

parking lot, most frozen in shock at the sight in front of them. Some of them were starting to scatter. I was backing my overpowered roadster through and around the mass of them, trying to speed away from the goo monster that was coming after us. Then I saw the large warehouse door was open, backed in and spun around.

I sped around pallets and a couple rows of shelves, all while the goo monster was still chasing us. I had the idea that I might go out another warehouse door, or barring that, head right through the storefront—an idea that didn't appeal to me. I had Kitty's paint job to think about, of course. And then, it happened.

We came to a dead end. Someone had left a pallet loader in the middle of an aisle with the fork extended. Shelves of microwaves on every side, there was no way out of this in the car. I made to get out of the car and run, but Glory stopped me.

She grabbed my right hand as I was reaching my left to the door handle. "I think I have a way out of this." She reached into her handbag and pulled out a doggy dish and handed it to me. "Put my neck in there after the explosion," she explained calmly.

"What?" I said—or exclaimed—I don't know how best to describe what I was thinking there. Nothing was making sense. All I know is that I was grabbing Glory's arm as she was trying to get out of the car. "What are you doing?" I asked.

"I'm going to stop that thing from following us," she answered. "Get ready to catch and drive."

I let go and watched her step out of the car and walk forward into the aisle between microwave boxes stacked fifteen feet high on each side of us. I don't know why I let her go. I suppose when a girl walks into your office and calmly removes her own head, you might start to think she's got a handle on the situation. She kept walking forward and was perhaps twenty feet in front of me when the goo monster came around the corner.

Glory just stood there, like a prize waiting to be won. She

knew that thing was after her and wouldn't bother with me. I couldn't help but think what a clod I was to just let her do this. I got out of the car, still unsure of her plan. The goo monster walked closer and reached forward. And that's when Glory tossed her head back to me. It was an amazing throw, coming straight at me. I was shocked, but was able to catch it. In a moment of lucidity with all the strangeness going on around me, I grabbed that doggy dish and put her neck in it. I could see now that there were some dials and buttons on the thing.

"Duck," I heard her whispering voice say as I was installing the head into the base. I looked up to see Glory's body glowing in the hands of the goo monster. I ducked back into the car as low as I could, and then the explosion happened.

It wasn't a boom so much as a sploosh and a clatter as the goo went everywhere and the office equipment holding it together in a somewhat humanoid-ish form fell loudly to the ground. I peeked my head up to see and the first thing I noticed was goo on the front end of my car.

"Dang it!" I burst out.

"What?" asked the head in my hands.

"Is that goo going to ruin my paint job?" I asked.

"Probably," she answered nasally, "but you have bigger problems to deal with."

"What's that?" I said as I started to notice exploded goo all over the floor, ceiling, and shelves of microwaves nearby.

"Your fingers are in my nose, for one."

I looked down and removed the offending fingers quickly. Disgusting. I lost track of how I was holding Glory's head in all of the commotion. I turned her head to look at me.

"Sorry about that," I said, wiping my fingers on a pocket square. I'd had to dress up for the commercial shoot, and I was still in my three piece.

She scrunched her nose as if trying to get rid of a sneezy itch and failed. She sneezed on my hand. "Sorry about that," she said. "But about that other problem…"

"What's that?" I asked distractedly. I was pulling some hand sanitizer out of the glove compartment.

"Look at the shelves again, Hughey."

I looked up as she asked. One by one, microwave boxes were lighting up and the goo on the outside of the boxes was glowing.

I watched in fascination as one little goo pile formed into the shape of a little man. It was about the size of a G.I. Joe that I played with as a kid, but it didn't take too long and it was standing up looking around. I knew instantly that it was looking for Glory.

"Dang, that thing doesn't stop, does it?"

"No, Hughey. It doesn't. And it's coming for me. That's why I have to leave. I need you to get me to my apartment, fast."

Other figures were coalescing on other boxes around and in front of me. I set Glory's head in the seat next to me and pulled the seat belt around the base as best I could.

"Go Hugo!" she implored. "I've got this."

I turned to gun it as I saw a claw extend from her base and grab onto the fabric below. Dang, first a new paint job and now fabric work. I had a feeling insurance wouldn't cover it.

I patted the dashboard comfortingly. "It will be all right Kitty. We'll get through this together." She didn't respond, of course. Kitty isn't very talkative.

The microwave shelves glowed behind me as I drove Kitty through the main aisle. I sensed movement behind me. I didn't turn to look, but I had a feeling that a small army of little goo men were following us as fast as their little goo legs could take them. Glory's stand extended up so she had a better view and she looked around.

"They're coming," she whispered next me as I whipped the car around a corner. I gripped the wheel a bit tighter and swept around another corner. That's when I saw them. Little goo men were trying to cut me off. They had taken a short cut through the shelves and were in our way. Luckily, the closest exit was closer than they were. I braked and turned, applied some juice and a bit of shimmy on the wheel, and we drifted around the corner.

As we emerged from a side door of the warehouse past a group of wide-eyed employees, I finally was able to shift into a higher gear and we took off. Behind me, little goo men jumped onto real men and... something happened. I didn't really see it. I was busy getting the heck out of there, but I heard Glory's gasp.

"Oh no!" she cried.

"What?" I asked as I sped out onto 28th, weaving in and out of cars in my path.

"They just, they just..."

"What happened, Glory?" I asked again.

You might wonder. Did I find it strange talking to a head on a stilt in the car seat next to me? What was my motivation—I mean, why was I still helping Glory out? With no body, she no longer had the hot factor in her favor.

To be honest, everything happened so fast, I was kind of just running on adrenaline. My first instinct is always to help out the less fortunate. That's why I have the resale shop and the massive sales every President's Day and Labor Day. I gotta help the public out when I see a need, right?

At any rate, the hot girl without a body next to me was rather alarmed—does that make her a hothead? Sorry, rambling. She was kind of freaking out, like back in my office. She was repeating herself again. I'm sure that if the girl could walk, she would have been walking circles in Kitty's floor pads.

I reached over and slapped her face again. I think she blinked and stammered a bit. I couldn't tell because I had to keep my eyes on the road and watch for little goo guys. It's not like Hawaii Five-O where people can drive down busy streets at eighty miles an hour while looking at their partner the entire time. I had to actually make sure that Kitty didn't get any more damage while we were escaping from the little army of goo dudes.

In a moment, Glory came out of her catatonia. Her response was similar to the last time I slapped her. "Did you slap me?" She asked.

I didn't know what automatic responses a disembodied

head might have, but I didn't want to find out so I lied. "No," I said.

"Oh," she said with a disappointed voice. "I wonder how—"

"Glory," I interrupted. "You saw something back there as we left the warehouse. Can you share?"

I knew the cops were going to catch on to us soon. I couldn't keep going as fast as I had been on the busy Westport streets, so I slowed down to a more reasonable pace, hopeful that we had left the little army of goo behind us.

"Hugo, they ran into the crowd that was next to the building."

"Ok…" I started. "Did they keep coming after that?"

"No. Hugo, you don't understand. They ran *in* to the crowd. Every one of them ran inside of a person outside your building."

That couldn't be good. "They ran into people? Why would they do that?" I asked. I had a feeling I knew.

"Hugo, before we turned the corner, I saw three of your employees turn their heads and start running toward us, with their eyes glowing."

Dang. Now I was getting downright bothered. Possibly even irritated. Why? My girlfriend was no longer hot, my car was covered in toxic goo, the upholstery was ripped up, and I suffered a corporate takeover all in about ten minutes? That's just the start of my morning. I grumbled wordlessly as we kept driving. I don't know how Glory took that. She was strangely quiet.

I brought up the exploding body thing. I was having trouble figuring out what was next there. I mean, if you blow up your body does that mean you have a spare lying around? "So…" I started. "You blew up your body…"

"To save you from the goo monster."

"Thanks," I said distractedly. I wasn't sure it was really after me in the first place, though. "So what do you do now? Do you have a solution to your no-body problem?" I was a little concerned about our relationship at this point. I mean, how can one carry on a relationship with a head? Honestly, I'd been attracted to the package, not just the head. Does that make me shallow?

"Of course!" She smiled. "I always keep a spare body around in case of emergency."

I must admit, I didn't know how to take that. I was relieved and confused at the same time. How do you keep a spare body around anyway? I pondered that for a minute, and then I turned the corner into her apartment complex, the Casa de la Única. I'd dropped her off outside here a couple of times, but she hadn't invited me in yet. I now had a feeling there was probably something weird on the inside. I wasn't wrong.

Before I turned the car off, I reached for Glory's head from the passenger side where the claws were disengaging from the fabric of the seat. I managed to turn off the car and exit while holding Glory's head like a football under my right arm.

"I like your deodorant," Glory said sweetly.

I looked down. Her face was still beautiful. I smiled back, not sure if I was really feeling it. "Thanks, Baby. Now, which way to your place?"

"I'm apartment 114," she directed. "Go past the swamp monster's place and take the stairs on the left. Try to ignore the Amazon women in 108 through 113. We'll get sucked into a different story if we get too close."

"Too close? Like what?" I asked, getting confused again.

"Just don't go in their apartments. They have some deal about wanting to conquer the world through some massive brainwashing scheme. You should be fine if you avoid going in. Vinny does a good job of protecting me when I'm here, but he doesn't go in the apartments."

"Vinny?" I asked.

"Look up."

All I saw was a very large tomato vine that crept all along the edge of the roofline. "The tomato?" I asked.

"Yes. You should introduce yourself."

"To a tomato plant?" I asked incredulously. I looked down at the head held securely in my right arm and turned it so I could look Glory in the eyes.

She winked back. "It's only polite, Hughey. Here, I'll introduce you."

"Hey, Vinny," Glory called out. "What's going on?"

"Hey Glory," the vine responded… somehow. "I'm just hanging around. Nessie fed me a leprechaun today, so I'm feeling kind of full."

"Oh, really!" she exclaimed in an excited voice. "Did it taste good?"

"Like a pot of golden goodness in every bite," the vine responded.

"Oh, you don't say," Glory said.

"Yeah. He came with this shiny belt buckle over here." I could see it—a golden buckle next to an unusually large tomato a few steps down the vine. "I guess now it's my lucky charm."

Glory smiled with approval. "Well, I suppose that's better than the mermaid you had a couple weeks back."

"Yeah," the tomato vine responded. "Seafood. Bleh! Whoever thought a tomato would enjoy that, I don't know."

I could see Glory purse her lips suspiciously, but she changed the subject.

"Hey Vinny," she said. "I want to introduce you to my friend Hugo."

"Is this a new body for your collection?" the vine asked.

"Collection?" I asked.

I could tell Glory was trying to shake her head. All she was managing was a neck wiggle. "No! Don't be silly. He's my boyfriend."

"Isn't he a bit big to be a boy?" the vine asked. I don't know how it could tell. I didn't see any eyes.

"Vinny," she protested. "Boyfriend is a word that means he is special to me."

"Ooooh, like Leprechauns are special to me?"

"No, no. I'm not going to eat him." She glanced back at me. I could tell this conversation was going nowhere.

"Well, Vinny, it's really good to meet you," I said, trying to figure out a way to gracefully exit this situation. "Glory needs to get to her spare body in the apartment. Can we talk to you later?"

"Sure, sure!" the vine responded. "Do you happen to have any cats with you?"

"Uh, no. No cats."

"Oh darn. I love cats. I mean, they taste great. I could give up leprechauns altogether if I could just get a cat…"

The vine kept going on and on about how yummy cats were. Glory whispered that we should just head to the apartment. "When he starts talking about cats," she explained. "He's lost for a good half hour or so."

We walked up to the apartment door and I stopped. "Do you happen to have a key on you?" I asked Glory.

"No. I just tell the door that I'm here," she explained. "AQUI!" She said loudly, and the door opened.

"It's a Spanish-themed apartment complex," she said as we walked in the apartment. I'm sure that explained everything.

We walked into a rather ordinary looking apartment with a living room just inside the front door. I could see two worn out old La-Z Boy chairs, a leather ottoman, a TV and a Wii console. To the right was a galley kitchen.

"Well, do you like it?" Glory asked.

I looked around. It was so ordinary I didn't know what to say. "Uh, like what?" I said.

"It's my spaceship," she replied. "The apartment manager, a big ugly guy with an Eastern European accent named Frank, let me park it right inside my apartment."

So that's it. My girlfriend as good as told me she's an alien. After the morning we had, that made sense. Still, I didn't know what to think at the moment. "I don't see a spaceship," I told her.

"It's right in front of you, silly." I looked out at the living room. I supposed that a pair of La-Z Boy chairs and the Wii console could be the control center of a space ship if given enough imagination.

I scratched my head, wondering for a moment why I was

here. Somehow, Glory had become an all-important force in my life in the last few months. When she showed up to my commercial shoot earlier, I had been ready to do anything to help, and it felt like I had been going along with a conditioned response. Girlfriend is in trouble = help however needed.

When the girlfriend removed her head, I became curious. When the girlfriend blew up her body, I understood her act of sacrifice. When she asked me to take her head back to her place, well, of course! Why wouldn't I, right? I gotta help the girl out, I guess. I mean, some evil doctor dude is after her for some unknown reason and we're being chased by some unstoppable goo monster.

Somehow this wasn't adding up for me. I mean, sure, I get the whole actual moving around and talking head on a plate thing, but what was I really doing here? Here... where a spaceship is parked in her living room... disguised as a living room?

"Hughey?" Glory called in her sweetsy voice. Man, that voice always used to get me right in the gut. I'd be ready to crash through walls for that voice. Now?

I looked around again, regaining my bearings. "Uh huh," I answered. "I guess it looks pretty good," I told her.

"Thanks! So, can you take me back to the bedrooms?" she asked in that sugary voice again.

"Is that where your spare is?" I asked, looking down at her head cradled in my arm.

"Yes, and more," she said.

The sweet talk wasn't working for me, but I wasn't going to let her know that right then. I did feel a responsibility to help her out of her jam, so I decided to go along with it. At least get the head connected to the spare. Then I could get out and get some space to think. I didn't know where the goo guys were, but I knew they really weren't my problem. They were after Glory for some reason, and if she had a spaceship in her living room, I was sure she could take it from there.

I took her down the hallway, around the corner, and opened the door into a room that took my breath away. It was very cold. I could see ice forming on many of the machines nearby. Several machines held long clear tubes about the size of a coffin, and inside each of these coffin tubes was a body, sans head.

I was fascinated. I couldn't believe what I was looking at. I walked through the room and counted five human bodies, each different. One was obviously athletically fit, while another one was very curvy. Another was shorter, while the last two had different skin tones. Off to one side I noticed a larger tube that held a headless gorilla body and yet another that held some sort of reptilian body.

"Well?" Glory asked after I'd made my circuit through the room.

"Uh, well what?" I asked.

"Which one would you like me to use?"

It was at this moment that something clicked into place in my head. Where had all these bodies come from? Was my girlfriend a killer? Or was she just a body snatcher? Whatever the answer was, I was not sure I wanted to know. I hesitated.

"Hughey?" she called up to me from the crook of my arm. "Hughey, it's okay."

The voice. It was that same voice. I could tell it was supposed to do something to me, but for whatever reason, it wasn't working. I tried not to let my body language give me away. I might be holding the head, but I was in her territory.

So I pointed. I don't even remember which one I pointed at—it might have been the athletic one. It didn't matter really. I just needed to move this along.

"Okay then," Glory said. "Do me a favor, sweetie. Could you set me on that table over there and then give me a few minutes to freshen up? After that, who knows?"

Shivers ran up my spine. And not the good ones. I smiled back. "Sure, baby. Take all the time you need." I set her on the table and retreated to the front rooms. I looked around the living room, so ordinary in contrast to the ice chest of horrors I had just left. I still didn't see how that room could be a space ship in disguise. I walked straight to the door with the intention of walking out.

The only problem was that I couldn't leave. I turned the door handle and an automatic reply came out of a speaker next to the door.

"ACCESS DENIED. ACCESS IS ONLY PERMITTED TO AUTHORIZED PERSONNEL."

I tried again and achieved the same result.

Dang. I looked around, trying to see if there was anything I could use to my advantage. I tried turning on the TV, what I assumed was the control panel for the space ship. It turned out to work exactly like a TV. I turned on a baseball game and tossed the remote aside. I tried the Wii, but that acted completely normal as well.

Those possibilities exhausted, I went to the kitchen and rummaged around looking for something. I managed to slide a paring knife into my pocket, and noticing for the first time that I was thirsty, I opened the fridge.

As soon as I did, four heads turned to look at me.

"Is he supposed to be doing that?" one of them asked another.

"No," the other one replied and then addressed me. "Close the door and await instructions."

I closed the door of the fridge and stared at it. Well, I didn't know what kind of party the heads were having, but I was still thirsty. I opened it again and grabbed a Gatorade and some vodka out of the door and closed it before the officious broad head could order me around again.

I drank a few sips of Gatorade and then filled the bottle with the vodka. I took another sip. Yep. That did it.

I tipped it back to take another drink when Glory came into the room. "Oh, there you are, Hughey. I'm so glad you didn't get away."

I took another sip and set my drink down, smiling over at her. "I couldn't leave," (true) "without you, Baby," (Also true) "I've been looking forward to seeing you all together again." (complete lie)

"Ah, yes. Well, Doctor Chicago is still after us, and we'd

better get out of here."

Again, I wasn't convinced he was really after "us," but I was not going to argue that at that moment.

"Okay, Baby. Whatever you say. Can't we just use your spaceship?"

She laughed, leaving me confused. "You wouldn't fit in the fridge, silly!"

Oh! Now it made sense. The refrigerator was the ship, not the living room. Or maybe it didn't make sense. I don't know. I was pretty confused. What sense does it make to fly around in a refrigerator? Maybe about as much sense as flying around in a telephone booth?

"So, what do you think we should do?" I asked.

"I've got a place just outside of town," she said. "We should hurry."

I grabbed her new hand as we started for the door, and an immediate feeling of relaxation came over me. Now that I was aware that I was being manipulated, every sensation around her was suspect. I needed to ditch her as quickly as possible, before her sweetsy voice took control of me all over again.

Before we took three steps, the front door burst open. Several of my employees rushed in, eyes glowing and covered in goo. They surrounded us as another figure entered. He was tall with sparse hair, strange goggle-glasses, and a grey lab coat.

"Aha! I have you at last!" he exclaimed triumphantly as he skidded to a stop in front of Glory.

Glory struggled in the grasp of her captors. Somehow a button came undone on her blouse. Her blonde hair whipped from one side to the other as her captors held on to her arms. "How did you find us?" she demanded through clenched teeth.

"Ah! But you led me right here, my pretty one!" he exclaimed again. "Elements of my creatures adorn your vehicle outside! It was, but a simple thing to follow, their signal to your abode, my dear." The doctor seemed very emphatic about everything he did, as if he was a hack actor or William Shatner was overacting his part.

He pulled a tomato out of a pocket and dramatically took a

bite.

"Yumm! What a tasty tomato! I wonder how you grow such large meaty tomatoes…" he trailed off with a sad expression. "Alas, there will be no more." Outside the open door, we could both see the charred remains of Vinny.

Glory struggled even more. Her blonde hair continued to whip from side to side while her body gyrated in the grasp of Doctor Chicago's minions. "You'll never get away with this, you, you…"

Doctor Chicago smiled just inches from her face and stroked her chin. "Ah, but I already have, my dear. There is no way to escape my minions." He turned to me. "And you. You are an interesting conundrum. An interesting one indeed. Do you know what they plan for you?"

"Stop!" Glory cried. A goo-laden employee grabbed her and pulled her back. Some goo oozed over Glory's mouth and covered it so that she could no longer speak.

Doctor Chicago turned back to me, his squinty eyes squinting even squintier. He began to intone something very softly.

"They come for the kings, the leaders of men,
the men that others both love and dread.
Throughout all time and through all space,
they hunt for them and they take their—"

"Wait, how does that go again? I can never remember that line."

"Heads?" I supplied.

"HEADS! That's it! Wait, how did you know that?" The doctor looked thoroughly confused.

"It rhymes?" I said.

"Really? Well, bully for you. At any rate, they come find the great leaders of men and take their heads. King Louis of France, Elvis, King Charles of England…"

"Wait," I protested. "Elvis wasn't a king."

"Sure he was. He was the king of rock and roll," he said while gyrating his hips. "And before you ask about Charles, don't. Sometimes these girls don't make a lot of sense."

"Like me?" I supplied.

"Well, I don't know enough about you yet to make a decision, Mr. King. I'm going to have to hold on to you until I know more."

I looked over at the still struggling Glory. I could hear her muffled cries. I just didn't have a lot of empathy for them at the moment. She had been after my head after all. "What do you plan with her?" I asked.

"Her? The headhuntresses have a chemical in their brains that I need to stabilize my super-goo soldier formula. As soon as I can get my hands on a supply of that, I can rule the world!" He waltzed over to the fridge and peeked inside. "And I've hit the motherload!" he exclaimed excitedly.

"Now, we'll have to put you on ice to get you back to my lab…" He turned, pointed a gun at me and fired.

.

.

.

.

.

.

.

.

.

.

.

.

.

.

.

.

.

.

.

.

.

You didn't think that was the end, did you? Sorry. I had to take a drink there while I was driving. My throat gets pretty dry when I'm driving Kitty with the windows down.

So that gun that the doctor pointed at me wasn't a real gun. It was just a tranquilizer gun meant to knock me out. It did the trick, but my eyes were only closed a few seconds when Kitty made her entrance.

I was fading off into sleepy sleepy land when Kitty burst through the front of the apartment, bouncing the TV and ottoman off her hood and knocking Doctor Chicago to the ground. In a burst of light, she transformed into a cat-woman and crawled up on top of Doctor Chicago. He turned over weakly and she hissed and batted at the side of his head with her paw, knocking him out. I witnessed all of this through half-closed eyes that I struggled to keep open.

Her feline ears pricked up and she peered over at me, her gaze going through me as if searching my soul. Leaving Doctor Chicago, she slinked over to me and extended one needle-tipped claw toward my arm. I felt a prick just as I was fading out again. Yes, my cat-woman bodyguard comes equipped with antivenin in her claw. Doesn't yours?

It wasn't long before I snapped out of my funk. I gave Kitty a scratch on the neck before I quickly turned my attention to my goo-covered employees. I concentrated on them. The ones that surrounded me dropped their arms and stared blankly ahead. Then I directed the ones around Glory to remove her head. I sent one of the employees to the back bedroom to get the base for her head and we set it in. That was when I allowed the gag to come off.

"Hugo!" she commanded. "What are you doing? Stop this!"

"You don't control me, Glory." I explained to her.

"What? How? I always control my man!"

"I think you blew your control when you blew up your body," I said. "As we drove here, my senses started to come back as your control wore off. I figured things out before Chicago ever showed up."

"But how are you controlling the goo men? Who's that on top of Doctor Chicago?"

"Oh, you don't know who you were after, do you? I'M THE KING, Glory. Kitty is more than a car and more than a cat. She is liege-bound to me. As for the goo men, well, they splattered all over MY microwaves, so I control them now."

"WHAT?" she screamed. "Do you mean to tell me that you could have stopped the goo monster at any time?"

I shrugged. "I was curious."

As an aside here, I fully intended to free my employees of the mind-controlling goo as soon as we could get them away from this place. The less they consciously know about the events of the day, the better. The truth is really very simple. My stores are my domain. Whatever happens there is never out of my ultimate control. It had been that way since the days of my grandfather. We never figured out why, but the King family were truly masters in their tiny corner of the world.

I suspect that Glory and her kind knew something more about that than I did. As far as I'd known up to today, I was the only living person who was aware of my ability. However, as the malevolent Doctor Chicago said, they go after the men of power. There had to be something to that, I just don't know what.

As to the power itself, I can't control people's buying choices, but I can control a lot of other things. I make the choice to make my store a good place for my employees as my daddy taught me and as his daddy taught him.

Glory spluttered a little and got red in the face. "I'll never live this down!" She pouted. "The girls will put my head in a locker for a year once they rescue me. And then…"

I stopped her there. "They won't rescue you, Glory. I'll make sure of that."

Her mouth stopped working and she stared at me with all the vehemence that her little head could muster. "You're not going to kill me."

"Nope. But I'm not the head cheese for nuthin. Doris is going on maternity leave soon and I'll need a new head secretary. I think keeping you close will be the best thing I can do."

43

Glory's lip turned down into that little pout she does when she's trying to get her way. "And why would I do that for you?"

I pointed at the fridge. "Because your sisters in the fridge are about to go into the R&D department. I don't think you'll be seeing them again for a really long time. But, rest assured, if you try anything, I can always take one of the girls out for batting practice.

Her eyes narrowed and I felt a tickle in the back of my head. She tried her sweetsy voice once again. "Come on, Hughey. We can come to an arrangement."

HA! I thought really hard. Glory looked as if she'd been slapped.

"Your headhunting days are over Glory, unless I ever allow you into the Human Resources Department. Now, you're going to tell me all about this base you have outside of town. What's it for? How did you expect to be able to protect yourself from Doctor Chicago?

I picked up Glory's head and walked out the door as she reluctantly began her explanation. Kitty followed close behind.

Later that day, my top manager Tom came over to Casa de la Unica and bought the place for me. I had Doctor Chicago moved to corporate headquarters. He'll make a fine addition to the staff. The Amazon women will be absorbed into the team as well. I have an inkling that they'll be a great addition to the sales team. And Vinny the tomato vine? He's actually ok, if in a reduced capacity. I'll have him transplanted in the alley behind the resale shop. He should find a new and interesting feast there. He'll be as good as new in no time.

We're driving now to find this place outside of town she was telling me about. I need to know about all the threats that my citizens face, after all. Glory's a bit cranky about it and wants to get it over with. I think she still fears I might kill her. I really don't need to, so I'll keep her around.

So, yeah. that's my adventure for the day. I think I'll drop the top, take a sip… aah… and ride toward that sunset now. Yeah, that'll do.

"Hugo! Stay on the ROAD!"

~*~

The Lost Tapes–Jack Carter

Daniel Arthur Smith

~*~

"RECORDING BEGINS WITH TODAY'S DATE, MAY 22^(ND), 2017. My name is Agent Melissa Muldoon. Present with me is Agent Lawrence Meyer. Commencing interview of one Professor Jack Carter. Professor Carter, can you please state your name for the record?"

"Um…Right in here?"

"Where you're sitting is fine. The device can pick you up."

"Okay. My name is Jack Carter."

"Thank you, Professor."

"It's quite all right."

"And thank you for coming in. I'm sure it's a rough time."

"A rough time?"

"At the university."

"Oh yes, yes. It's all so upsetting."

"What is your role there?"

"At the university?"

"At the university."

"I'm a researcher."

"Could you please clarify Professor?"

"Yes. Of Course. I'm researcher at the Stem Cell Research Institute."

"You founded the institute?"

"Yes...Yes, I did. That's correct."

"Yet you look so young. How old are you Professor Carter?"

"I'm forty-five."

"A bit young to be the founder and lead of a university institute."

"I started young."

"What kind of research do you do there?"

"We perform a wide range of study. Everything from organ reparation to cancer treatments."

"You specifically please."

"I'm a professor of regenerative biology."

"Regenerative biology?"

"Yes."

"That's quite impressive."

"It sounds exciting I'm sure, but the day to day..."

"Just what is the day to day?"

"Well...My work is mostly administrative. Designing protocols. Peer review."

"Plus the work in the lab."

"Well, to be truthful, the students do most of the work in the lab."

"The students."

"Phd students. They monitor the protocols the lead researchers, such as myself, have designed. My time is taken up in peer review and publishing the results."

"Can you identify the person in the photo?"

"Oh my. It's her."

"I know this is disturbing, but can you please name this person?"

"That's Miss Blake, Emily Blake."

"For the record, Professor Carter has identified the deceased as twenty-four-year-old female, Emily Blake.

"Mr. Carter Was Emily Blake one of those students?"

"Yes, she was. Miss Blake was my research assistant."

"What duties did Miss Blake perform?"

"Monitor protocols, as I said. She—like the other Phd

students— collected and recorded the findings."

"When did you last see her?"

"I saw Miss Blake yesterday, when I went to collect the reports."

"And what time was that?

"Midday."

"Can you be more specific?"

"Before lunch. 11:30, I suppose. I collected the reports, had lunch, and then collated them in the afternoon."

"At your office?"

"My home office."

"Is that typical to work at home?"

"In the afternoons. Sometimes into the evening."

"Can you can tell me what parabiosis is?"

"Certainly. The union of two organisms to allow sharing of circulation systems. It's an antiquated idea."

"How so?"

"It was believed that if two organisms were joined, like conjoined twins, that their joined circulation would provide beneficial factors."

"I read something on the internet. Here, I printed it out. It says, 'a young mouse and an old mouse were sewn together, their veins conjoined, and the older mouse became younger.'"

"It's ridiculous. Quackery really. Why do you ask?

"Emily Blake wrote about in her journal."

"Her journal?"

"Yes. We have her bullet journal. She kept rather detailed notes, on her daily activity, her water intake, exercise regime, and on a parabiosis experiment."

"I assure you that the institute is not conducting any lab experiments that involve joining organisms. If the students were conducting experiments with the mice, it was not under the auspices of the institute or universities."

"Let me see—she even put an index in the front—here it is. 'Of the hundred bio-markers in the blood, none seem to have the anti-aging benefits as the protein growth factor GDF11.' Professor do you know what she's talking about here?"

"Not really. I know what GDF11 is, but I don't know her context."

"The context. It seems, from what I found on the internet, that there is another form of parabiosis, other than joining bodies. It's through blood transfusion. That seems to be the type of parabiosis experiment Emily wrote about in her journal."

"It is?"

"It is. Would you like to hear more?"

"I suppo—"

"She writes, 'As there is more GDF11 in younger people, their blood has the most benefits. I believe that is why he wants my blood.' Professor. Who do you think he is?"

"I wouldn't know."

"Emily was so detailed. Every glass of water gets a little x in a box. She has her menstrual cycle detailed, and she has the blood transfusions, several of them spaced out, with notes as to what she ate, before and after."

"It's the nature of our work. To document."

"Is it? I guess it is. Mine too. You know I keep a bullet journal. Two journals, actually. One as a personal diary. Which had me thinking that she probably had a second journal. And, guess what we found when we searched her apartment? A personal journal. A diary. And this woman, I must say, had a lot to write about you."

"She did?"

"Oh yes. She had a deep crush on you. In her last entry, from the night before last, she wrote, 'He makes me want to be my best, drives me to be my best, mentally, physically, he wants what's best for me. Tomorrow, after the treatment, I'll tell Jack that I love him.'...Did she?"

"Did she what?"

"After the treatment, which by the way, cross referenced with her bullet journal was a blood transfusion at 11:30—after the transfusion, did she confess her love for you? Is that why you strangled her? Killed her?"

"You don't understand. She became upset when I rejected her. It's improper. She is...was my assistant. Our relationship has boundaries."

"And for that you killed her? No. I think there is more to it. She knew something about you. And when you rejected her, she threatened to tell."

"No, again, you don't understand."

"I don't think you understand. Can you identify the man in this black and white photo?"

"No. No I cannot."

"I'd say he looks like you. In fact, I'd say he looks like you in a costume. What do you say, Larry? That means Agent Meyer agrees."

"It's not me."

"Maybe it is. Maybe it's not. Probably not. But coincidentally, this man was a Professor, too. From right here at the university. His name was Jacque Cartier. We have this photo on file because he too lost a research assistant. Do you recognize this photo?"

"No. I don't."

"That is the medical examiner's photo of Molly Shea, Jacque Cartier's research assistant. She died of strangulation, the same as Emily Blake and get this—exsanguination, same as Emily. Both of them had the blood drained from them. But that's not the strangest part. Molly died in 1882."

"I believe I'll need a lawyer."

~*~

ABOUT THE AUTHORS

D.K. Cassidy scribbles daily in various genres including Science Fiction, Magical Realism, & Urban Gothic. Her goal? Messing with your mind by transforming the voices in her head into odd stories.

She lives in the Pacific Northwest with her greatest fans: her husband Mark, twin sons Aidan and Jared, and four cats. When not writing, she loves to travel, run, knit, use the Oxford comma, and of course read!

For more information, visit dkcassidy.com

Jason LaVelle is an author and photographer from West Michigan. When he's not spending time with his beautiful wife and four children, he's probably at the dog park with his three pugs, Dragon, Dylan and Mr. Sparkles and his annoying dachshund, Lady. After he's done playing with the pugs and tucking the kids into bed, he explores the paranormal world through his writing.

Jon Frater is a librarian at MCNY. He writes science fiction and fantasy in his spare time and is preparing to release Book 1 of his new Expocalypse Weird series.

He lives in New York with his wife and children.

Paul K. Swardstrom is a husband and a father, a music teacher by day and family man at night.

A Sun Devil who grew up all over but remembers Michigan fondly, I have settled in Oregon.

Daniel Arthur Smith is the author of the international bestsellers *Hugh Howey Lives*, *The Cathari Treasure*, *The Somali Deception*, and a few other novels and short stories. He also curates the phenomenal short fiction series *Tales from the Canyons of the Damned*.

He was raised in Michigan and graduated from Western Michigan University where he studied philosophy, with focus on cognitive science, meta-physics, and comparative religion. He began his career as a bartender, barista, poetry house proprietor, teacher, and then became a technologist and futurist for the Fortune 100 across the Americas and Europe.

Daniel has traveled to over 300 cities in 22 countries, residing in Los Angeles, Kalamazoo, Prague, Crete, and now writes in Manhattan where he lives with his wife and young sons.

For more information, visit danielarthursmith.com

~*~

www.ingramcontent.com/pod-product-compliance
Lightning Source LLC
Chambersburg PA
CBHW020319150626
46552CB00022B/3002